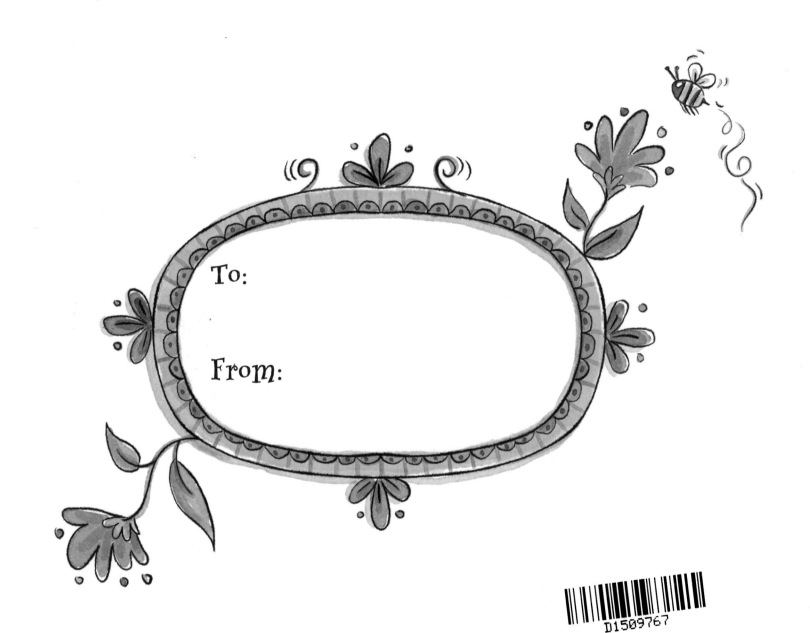

To:

From:

D1509767

DEAR GRANDMA

by *New York Times* Bestselling Author and Illustrator

Susanna Leonard Hill & John Joseph

sourcebooks
wonderland

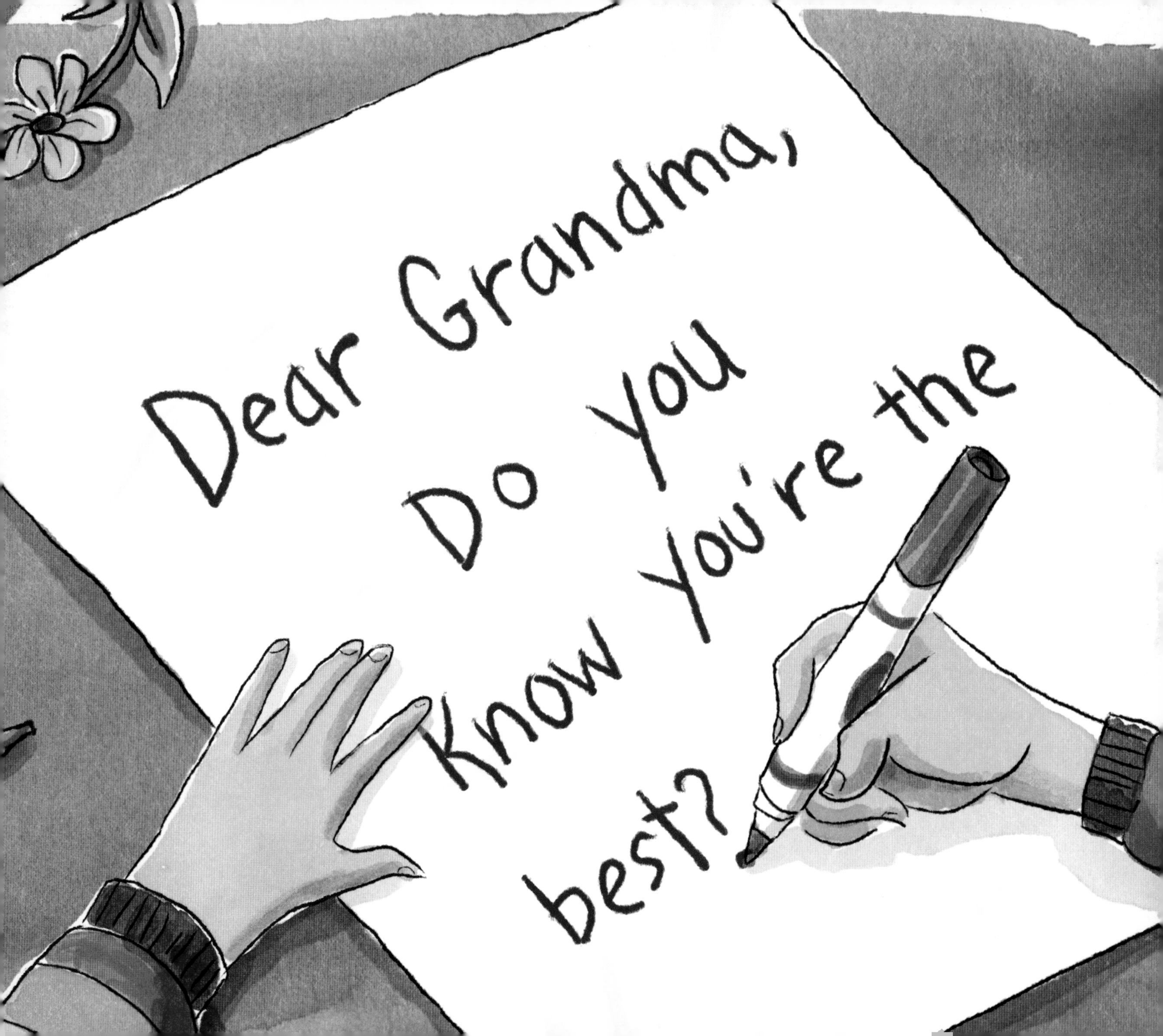
Dear Grandma,
Do you
know you're the
best?

You're grab pots and pans,
let's make a band,
cheer up and bake
a rainy Saturday cake…

Push the furniture aside and take a magic carpet ride!

You're a jungle gym climber, jump rope rhymer,
storyteller, secret hideout dweller,
snack sneaker, costume tweaker,
super-duper hide 'n' seeker.

You're all kinds of fun, rolled into one!

But Grandma, you're so much more.
You're a bad day eraser,
nightmare chaser…

Fight ender,
  problem mender,
    kick off your shoes and dance away the blues.

Take a walk so we can talk,

    hold my hand and understand

that sometimes things don't go as planned.

Everybody makes mistakes,
    but you say I've got what it takes

to right what's wrong, stay strong, and face whatever comes along.

Grandma, you always make things better.
You wipe my saddest tears away,
and say,

"Dear one, you'll be okay."

When I feel scared and want to run,
you shout, "Look out trouble! Here we come!"
We're fist shakers, peacemakers,
fear beaters, dragon defeaters!

You're summer seasides,

winter sled rides,

springtime
puddles,

autumn cuddles.

All year long,
we're two halves
of a whole.

It seems like everywhere we go

you teach me things I didn't know,

and as I grow, there's more we'll share,

because near or far, you're always there.

You're follow your star,
be who you are.
You let me feel free just to be ME,
and you always love completely.

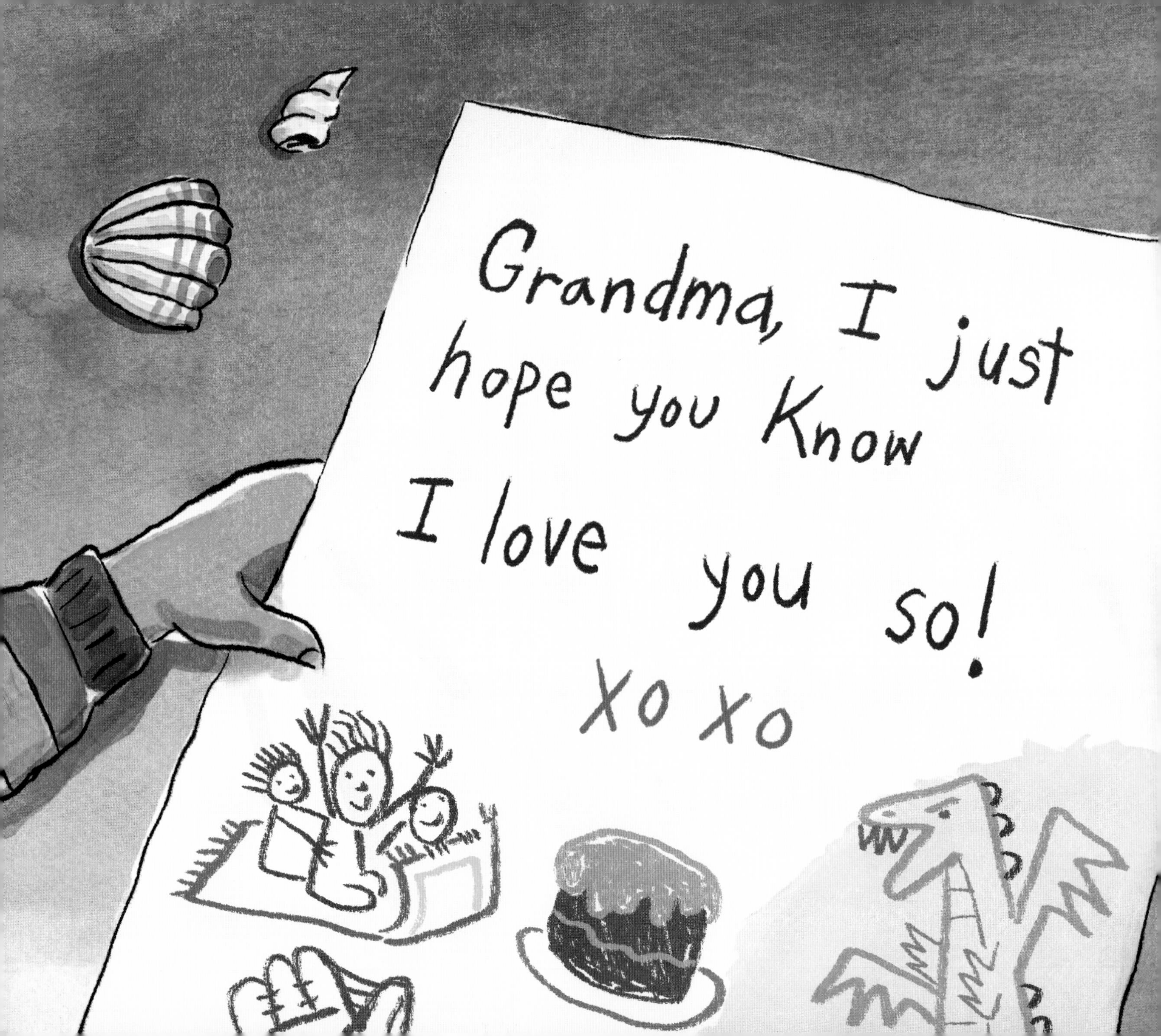
Grandma, I just hope you Know
I love you so!
XO XO

For all grandmas, cookie bakers, sweater makers, sky divers, motorcycle
drivers, strong, smart, full of heart—and the grandchildren who love them so!
—SLH

To Grandma, G-Ma and Yaya, the best grandmas any kid could hope for!
—JJ

The full color art was prepared both digitally and using traditional watercolor.

Published by Sourcebooks Wonderland, an imprint of Sourcebooks Kids
P.O. Box 4410, Naperville, Illinois 60567–4410
(630) 961-3900
sourcebookskids.com

Library of Congress Cataloging-in-Publication Data is on file with the publisher.

Source of Production: 1010 Printing Asia Limited, North Point, Hong Kong, China
Date of Production: September 2020
Run Number: 5019409

Printed and bound in China.
OGP 10 9 8 7 6 5 4 3 2 1